This Topsy and Tim book belongs to

_____

This title was previously published as part of the *Topsy and Tim Learnabout* series
Published by Ladybird Books Ltd
80 Strand London WC2R ORL
A Penguin Company

1 3 5 7 9 10 8 6 4 2

Printed in Italy

Go on an Aeroplane

Jean and **Gareth Adamson**

Topsy and Tim were off on their
summer holidays. They were going
in an aeroplane.

The airport was very big.
Topsy and Tim had a long ride in a
bus to reach the terminal building.

Then they had a long ride on an escalator to get to the right part of the building.

Their luggage went
for a long ride too, on
a moving platform.

Topsy and Tim watched
an aeroplane land.
It looked much bigger when
it was not in the sky.

The door was high off the ground.
"How will the people get out?"
asked Topsy.

"Through a special tunnel," said Mummy. "You will see when it's our turn to get on the plane."

The loudspeaker voice announced that
Topsy and Tim's aeroplane was ready.
Soon they were walking along a
telescopic tunnel and stepping into the
aeroplane. It looked like a very long bus.

"Welcome aboard," said the
stewardess to Topsy and Tim.

The stewardess helped Topsy and Tim
fasten their safety belts.
She gave them some comics and
some sweets.

"Suck a sweet when the aeroplane starts to fly," she said. "It will stop your ears hurting."
Tim took two sweets.
"One for each ear," he said.
The stewardess laughed.
"They go in your mouth, not your ears!" she said.

The big aeroplane flew up into the sky.
Topsy and Tim watched trees and
houses grow as small as toys.
"My ears have gone funny,"
said Topsy.
"You didn't suck your sweet, that's
why," said Tim.

Topsy and Tim were flying above
the clouds.
"Isn't this exciting!" said Mummy.
But the clouds went on for miles
and miles.
Topsy and Tim began to fidget.

Lunch came in interesting plastic trays.
Each piece of food had its own shaped space like the pieces of a jigsaw puzzle. Topsy and Tim tried to swap pieces. The stewardess had to clear up the mess.
Then she said, "Topsy and Tim, the pilot would like to talk to you."

The stewardess took Topsy and Tim
to the pilot's cabin.
"Hello twins," said the pilot.
"I've been hearing about you."
He showed Topsy and Tim all the
switches and levers and dials he used
to fly the aeroplane.
"Do you think you could fly my
aeroplane?" asked the pilot.
Topsy and Tim were not sure.

They went back to their seats and
fastened their safety belts once more.
Then they pretended to be pilots.
"Will you land our aeroplane now,
please, pilots?" asked the stewardess.

Topsy and Tim could see the flaps
moving in the aeroplane's wings to
make it fly lower.
"I'm doing that when I move this
lever," said Tim. But Topsy and Tim
both knew the real pilot was doing it.

Topsy and Tim's aeroplane
landed with hardly a bump.

"Goodbye everybody," said Topsy and Tim.
They waved goodbye to the stewardess and to the pilot up in the aeroplane's nose. Then they went to meet their luggage on another moving platform.

And that is how Topsy and
Tim flew in an aeroplane.